SPEED MACHINES

HOVERCRAFT

BY MATT SCHEFF

SportsZone

An Imprint of Abdo Publishing
www.abdopublishing.com

www.abdopublishing.com

Published by Abdo Publishing, a division of ABDO, PO Box 398166,
Minneapolis, Minnesota 55439. Copyright © 2015 by Abdo Consulting Group,
Inc. International copyrights reserved in all countries. No part of this
book may be reproduced in any form without written permission from the
publisher. SportsZone™ is a trademark and logo of Abdo Publishing.

Printed in the United States of America, North Mankato, Minnesota
082014
012015

**THIS BOOK CONTAINS
RECYCLED MATERIALS**

Cover Photo: Marcel Jancovic/Shutterstock Images
Interior Photos: Marcel Jancovic/Shutterstock Images, 1, 14-15; Stocktrek Images/
Corbis, 4-5; Eric Risberg/AP Images, 6-7; Ian Woolcock/Shutterstock Images, 8-9; AP
Images, 10-11; Dean Conger/Corbis, 12-13; Shutterstock Images, 16-17, 18-19, 20-21,
28-29, 31; Charlie Neuman/ZUMA Press/Corbis, 22-23; Elaine Thompson/AP Images,
24-25; Jens Meyer/AP Images, 26; Scanpix Sweden/Pontus Lundahl/AP Images, 26-27

Editor: Chrös McDougall
Series Designer: Nikki Farinella

Library of Congress Control Number: 2014944187

Cataloging-in-Publication Data
Scheff, Matt.
 Hovercraft / Matt Scheff.
   p. cm. -- (Speed machines)
 ISBN 978-1-62403-610-1 (lib. bdg.)
 Includes bibliographical references and index.
 1. Ground-effect machines--Juvenile literature. 2. Hydrofoil boats--Juvenile literature.
 I. Title.
 629.3--dc23
                                                                    2014944187

CONTENTS

OVER WATER, OVER LAND

Sea water sprays up behind the spinning propeller blades of a US Navy hovercraft. It rushes toward a sandy beach where US troops wait for supplies. Jets of air shoot out of the bottom of the craft, keeping it above the water's surface.

A US Navy hovercraft cruises across the ocean.

FAST FACT

A fully loaded US Navy LCAC hovercraft can weigh more than 10 elephants!

The hovercraft doesn't have to slow down as it approaches land. The craft smoothly glides over the sand. What's beneath this versatile vehicle doesn't matter. The hovercraft can go over oceans, lakes, swamps, beaches, or fields. The hovercraft's pilot slows it to a stop and the troops unload the vehicle's supplies. Then it's right back out over the water for another trip!

A US Navy hovercraft moves from the water to the sand.

THE HISTORY OF HOVERCRAFT

Powerful engines blowing downward allow hovercraft to float just above the earth's surface. This seems like a futuristic concept, but people have been building vehicles that hover over land or water for decades. Early models needed to be moving to hover. During the 1950s, Charles J. Fletcher invented a vehicle called a glidemobile. But the US Army kept it top secret. In 1955, Christopher Cockerell built a vehicle prototype that floated on a cushion of blown air, even while at rest. He named it the hovercraft.

A hovercraft ferry arrives onshore in England.

9

FAST FACT

At first, the SR.N1 had no skirt. It could only hover about 1 foot (.3 m) high. So it worked only on calm water and at low speeds.

NRDC HOVERCRAFT SR

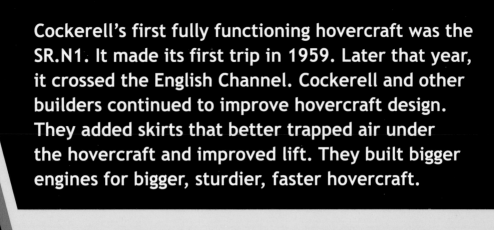

Cockerell's first fully functioning hovercraft was the SR.N1. It made its first trip in 1959. Later that year, it crossed the English Channel. Cockerell and other builders continued to improve hovercraft design. They added skirts that better trapped air under the hovercraft and improved lift. They built bigger engines for bigger, sturdier, faster hovercraft.

The SR.N1 hovercraft comes ashore in Kent, England, after crossing the English Channel in 1959.

The use of hovercraft quickly increased. Militaries around the world began to use them. US troops used them to patrol rivers and deltas during the Vietnam War. Other hovercraft became passenger vehicles. In 1968, large Mountbatten-class hovercraft began transporting people and cars across the English Channel.

FAST FACT

The first hovercraft race was held in 1964 in Canberra, Australia. More than 30,000 fans watched the race.

Most hovercraft have the same basic design.

PARTS OF A HOVERCRAFT

The modern hovercraft doesn't look much different from those built in the 1960s. They still have the same basic parts. The hovercraft starts with a simple, lightweight body. One or more engines sit on the back of the body. These engines power rapidly spinning fans.

FAST FACT

Some hovercraft can rise as high as 9 feet (2.7 m) off the ground!

A hovercraft races over water.

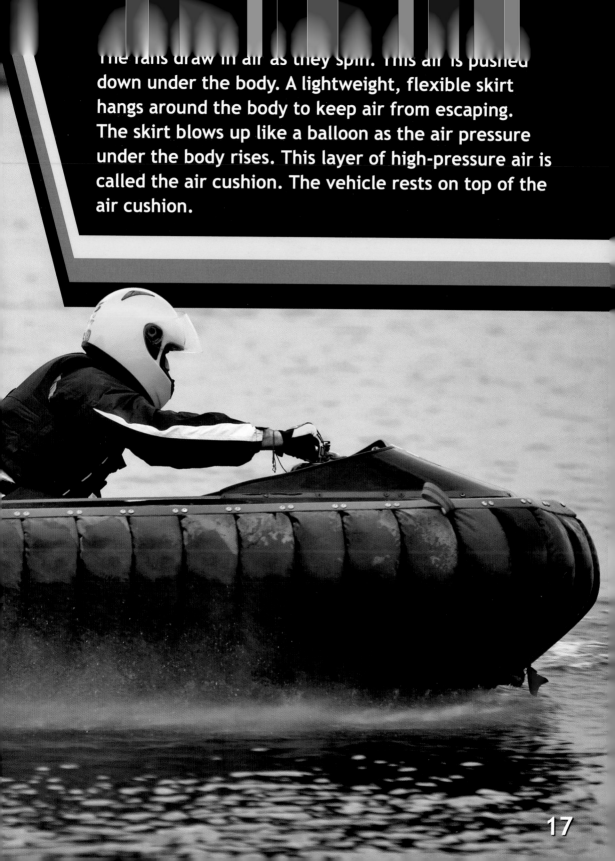

The fans draw in air as they spin. This air is pushed down under the body. A lightweight, flexible skirt hangs around the body to keep air from escaping. The skirt blows up like a balloon as the air pressure under the body rises. This layer of high-pressure air is called the air cushion. The vehicle rests on top of the air cushion.

Bob Windt holds the world record for hovercraft speed at 85.4 miles per hour (137 km/h).

92

RAVENOL

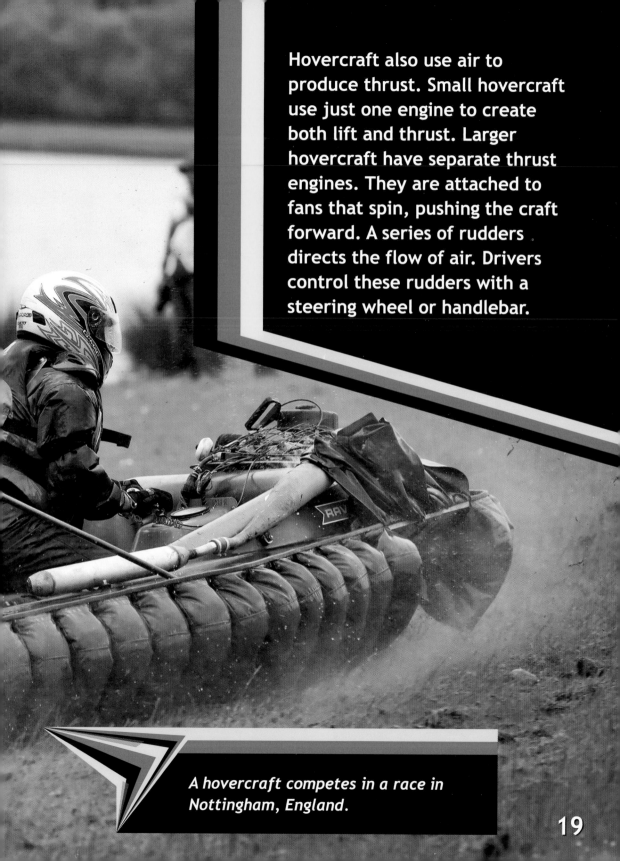

Hovercraft also use air to produce thrust. Small hovercraft use just one engine to create both lift and thrust. Larger hovercraft have separate thrust engines. They are attached to fans that spin, pushing the craft forward. A series of rudders directs the flow of air. Drivers control these rudders with a steering wheel or handlebar.

A hovercraft competes in a race in Nottingham, England.

PHOTO DIAGRAM

1. Body
2. Engine
3. Fan
4. Skirt
5. Air cushion
6. Cockpit/
   Steering Wheel
7. Rudder

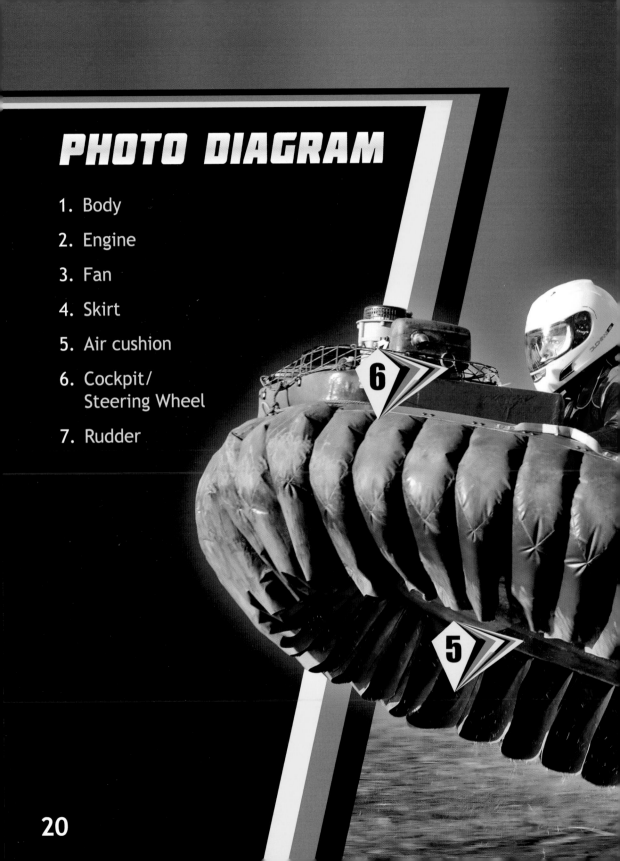

HOVERCRAFT IN ACTION

Modern hovercraft can go places other vehicles cannot reach. They can coast over oceans, lakes, and swamps. They can cruise over land. That makes them perfect landing craft for militaries. The biggest hovercraft can carry dozens of soldiers and all of their gear.

FAST FACT

The largest hovercraft can even carry heavy tanks.

A US Navy hovercraft rides in front of an aircraft carrier in San Diego, California.

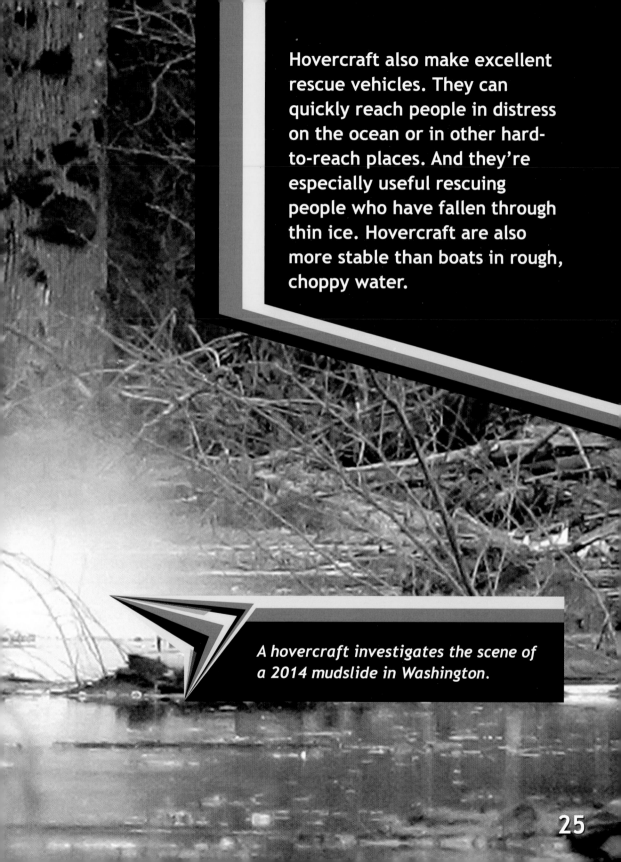

Hovercraft also make excellent rescue vehicles. They can quickly reach people in distress on the ocean or in other hard-to-reach places. And they're especially useful rescuing people who have fallen through thin ice. Hovercraft are also more stable than boats in rough, choppy water.

A hovercraft investigates the scene of a 2014 mudslide in Washington.

A hovercraft fights to maintain control during a Formula 1 race.

In recent years, hovercraft racing has become popular. Racers can enter their own hovercraft in all kinds of races. The top class of racing is with Formula 1 hovercraft. Formula 1 hovercraft have the biggest, most powerful engines. These vehicles tear around

Two hovercraft battle for position during a Formula 1 race in Sweden.

FAST FACT

Many of the top racers gather each year for the World Hovercraft Championship. The event is held approximately every two years.

Some small personal hovercraft are just for fun. Drivers love whipping their hovercraft over lakes, down dry riverbeds, and over sandy beaches. They enjoy taking their hovercraft to places no other vehicle could ever reach.

FAST FACT

You can buy a personal hovercraft for less than the price of a new car. But many owners like to build their own from scratch.

A hovercraft cruises down a canal in England.

GLOSSARY

deltas
Low-lying areas at the mouths of rivers.

hover
To remain in one place in the air.

landing craft
A vehicle designed to carry troops from water to land.

propeller
Blades that spin to propel a vehicle.

prototype
A first model of something, often built to show how future models could work.

rudder
A flat, hinged part that directs the flow of air out the back of a hovercraft; the rudder's position determines the direction the vehicle travels.

skirt
A lightweight, flexible band that encloses a hovercraft's air cushion.

thrust
Forward force produced by an engine.

versatile
Able to be used for various different functions.

FOR MORE INFORMATION

Books

Hanson, Anders. *Let's Go by Hovercraft*. Edina, MN: Abdo Publishing Co., 2008.

Tieck, Sarah. *Hovercraft*. Edina, MN: Abdo Publishing Co., 2011.

Voltz, Stephen. *How to Build a Hovercraft: Air Cannons, Magnet Motors, and 25 Other Amazing DIY Science Projects*. San Francisco: Chronicle Books, 2013.

Websites

To learn more about Speed Machines, visit **booklinks.abdopublishing.com**. These links are routinely monitored and updated to provide the most current information available.

INDEX

ABOUT THE AUTHOR

Matt Scheff is a freelance author and lifelong motor sports fan living in Minnesota.